Puppies

& Pet Crows

To Eric + Ryan
Have Fun with Louie!
Lou Hooker
2015

Puppies & Pet Crows

written by
LOU HOOKER

TATE PUBLISHING & Enterprises

Published by Tate Publishing & Enterprises, LLC
127 E. Trade Center Terrace | Mustang, Oklahoma 73064 USA
1.888.361.9473 | www.tatepublishing.com

Tate Publishing is committed to excellence in the publishing industry. The company reflects the philosophy established by the founders, based on Psalm 68:11,
"The Lord gave the word and great was the company of those who published it."

Book design copyright © 2011 by Tate Publishing, LLC. All rights reserved.
Cover and interior design by Chris Webb
Illustrations by Jason Hutton

Published in the United States of America

ISBN: 978-1-61777-200-9
1. Juvenile Fiction / Lifestyles / Farm & Ranch Life
2. Juvenile Fiction / Historical / United States / 20th Century
11.02.22

I dedicate this book to my dad and mom, Myreenus and Helene Hooker, who provided abundantly for my spiritual and physical life.

Other Books by Lou Hooker

Puppies and Pet Crows is book three of a series of books written by Lou Hooker, telling of his family living on a farm near Fremont, Michigan.

- Book 1: *The Year of the Fire,* 1941–1943
- Published by Louis Hooker
- ISBN: 978-0-9755106-0-5

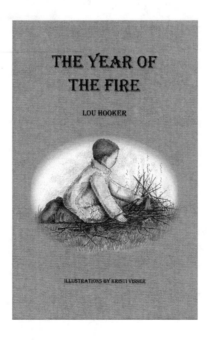

- Book 2: *Dog Days on the Farm,* 1943–1947
- Published by Louis Hooker
- ISBN: 978-0-9755106-1-2

- Book 3: *Puppies and Pet Crows* 1947–1948
- Published by Tate Publishing, LLC
- ISBN: 978-1-61777-200-9

Acknowledgments

Thanks, once again, to my talented wife, Verla, who tirelessly gave of her time to make this book a reality.

Thanks, Becky, my youngest daughter, for the helpful suggestions and editing.

I am grateful to my siblings, whose actions and words made these stories possible.

I also thank Jan Overzet for her careful editing and wise suggestions given.

Finally, I thank God, who makes all things possible.

Table of Contents

Big Bear

Grr! The sound that came from Louie's throat startled four-year-old Barbie, his youngest sister. But she responded with an enthusiastic, "Yes!"

The younger Hooker children knew what Louie meant by the sound and rushed to get their coats from the backroom. They were going to the barn to play Big Bear.

Louie lived in Western Michigan in a big white house on a farm with his dad and mum, four brothers, and three sisters.

It was December of 1947. Eleven-year-old Louie and his four younger siblings—Les, Corrine, Dale, and Barbie—rushed to the barn.

They scampered through the slushy snow.

Dad was milking the cows with his Sears milking machine. Brownie, the brown Swiss cow, turned her head as the five children ran behind her to the barn floor door.

The door to the barn floor went up two steps from the calf shed. Louie and his brothers fed the cows hay and cornstalks from the barn floor.

Barbie and Corrine stood nervously at the barn floor door. Les and Dale waited near the silo chute as Louie pushed the door open.

"You kids stay here while I go hide," Louie said.

He closed the door behind him so they couldn't see where he hid.

Louie looked at a spot behind the feed barrels. *No, that was too easy.* Then he saw some straw bales piled near the big barn doors. *No, they would look there right away.* He could hear one of the cows slurping water from her bucket. The bucket had a ring in the bottom that released water when she pushed it down with her nose.

Oh! I know! I'll squeeze myself into the soft, loose pile of hay, Louie thought.

He pulled his coat around his neck so the chaff would not get under his shirt and make him itch. Then he pushed the hay aside and dug his way under the sweet-smelling hay. He quickly made a hole in the backside, crawled in, and pulled the hay around him. No one would be able to see him. He was hidden.

"Forty-seven. Forty-eight. Forty-nine. Fifty. Let's go!" Les shouted.

"I'm scared!" Barbie cried. "The Big Bear is going to get me!"

"Oh, come on," Corrine said to Barbie. "This is just a fun game." But Corrine didn't tell Barbie that she shivered too, even though she knew what was going to happen.

Les and Dale went first. They walked carefully past the first mangers. Corrine and Barbie were right behind. Barbie clung to Corrine's pant leg.

"I think he went in the haymow up above," whispered Dale.

The four of them tiptoed toward the ladder that led to the haymow up above.

"*Grr!*"

"*Eek!*" they all screamed.

"Where did that sound come from?" Les yelled.

"Not up in the haymow, but down here somewhere!" Corrine shrieked.

"Listen!" Corrine shouted. "Let's all join hands so we can run fast to get away from Big Bear!"

Hand in hand, they tiptoed past the haystack to the far side of the barn floor.

"*Grr!*"

They all screamed and ran for the door.

Big Bear was right at their heels. He even touched Barbie and Corrine's shoulders, but they scurried through the door just in time to escape the grasp of Big Bear.

The Hooker kids played this game many times on winter evenings as Dad did the milking. Louie didn't hide just once, but five to ten times in one night.

Louie pulled his coat tightly around his neck as he and his brothers and sisters ran back to the house. Snow was blowing across the path.

Will there be school tomorrow? he wondered.

Blackie and Brownie

The next day was a snow day. No school. The wind blew all day on the Hooker farm. It made big drifts of snow between the house and the windmill.

Toward evening, the wind became quieter, and it stopped snowing.

Dad, Marve, and Harley busily milked the cows and did the evening chores. Marve and Harley were Louie's two older brothers. The rest of the family was in the house.

Louie looked out the window toward the windmill and saw the huge snow banks under the big willow tree. He ran to the backroom and put on his heavy coat, which was torn on the sleeve.

He grabbed a snow shovel that stood by the backdoor and hustled over to the big snow bank. He looked up at it. It was higher than his head. He touched the hard, cold mound with his mittened hand.

Louie thought, *I think I can make a snow house under this bank.*

He began digging carefully with the shovel.

Soon he had a large opening under the bank. He kept pushing the snow far out of the way from the opening. The snow was so stiff it didn't even cave in.

After much digging, he could sit up inside his snow room. Louie ran to the barn to tell his brothers about the house.

Brownie and Blackie, the family's two puppies, were snoozing on some straw. From their cozy pile of straw where they slept, Louie called, "Here, Brownie! Here, Blackie! Come!"

They eagerly scurried after Louie across the driveway, past the milk house, and toward Louie's snow house. Blackie got behind as he bounced along and let out a scared "*yip!*" Louie picked him up and carried him as Brownie followed at his heels. Louie bent down on his hands and knees to crawl through the snow doorway.

The curious puppies sniffed at the cold, snowy walls. They began shivering.

"Oh, you poor puppies. You don't have a heavy coat like me," Louie said.

An idea popped into his head. He ran to the house and filled a dishpan with hot water from the little kitchen sink. This room was called the little kitchen because in the past it had a cook stove for canning.

Louie sneaked the water out of the house and brought it to his snow house. He placed the steaming water in the center of his snow room. Curious, Blackie and Brownie soon sniffed the hot vapor and lapped some of the water.

The puppies were still shivering, so Louie unbuttoned the front of his big coat and tucked the puppies inside. Then he buttoned the coat. Close to Louie's tummy, the now-warm puppies soon fell fast asleep.

For a time, Louie felt very cozy inside his own little house, but soon, cold seeped through his coat and into his bones.

Shortly after, his brothers and dad came from the barn to the house for supper. Louie brought the pups inside the house where it was very warm and comfortable.

He placed them in the little kitchen in a cardboard box.

After supper, Louie showed his snow house to his younger brothers and sisters. They had to take turns crawling inside.

That night, as Louie lay in his bed, he thought about the fun snow day he had enjoyed on the farm. He couldn't wait until the day they could go sledding at Cousin Hank's gully. Tomorrow would be a school day again. The storm was over, but he knew there would be more snow days before the end of winter.

Sledding

It snowed a lot that winter. There was over two feet of snow on level ground. Snow didn't keep Louie and his brothers from going outside.

Saturday morning, Louie suggested to Harley, "Let's go sliding at the gully this afternoon."

"It's pretty cold outside, but we can dress warm," Harley answered.

Les added, "I'd like to go too. I can walk a long ways."

The boys would have to walk across the field to Cousin Hank's place and the gully.

Virginia served some good, hot pea soup for dinner at noon. Virginia was Louie's oldest sister. The boys ate heartily. Virginia said it would help keep them warm.

After dinner, Harley said, "Louie, get the Norge tin out of the shed." It was called the Norge tin because it was the side of a Norge refrigerator that had been torn apart. It made an excellent sliding tin.

The boys walked across the crusty snow to the east. Harley and Les pulled sleds, and Louie dragged the Norge tin.

When they arrived at Cousin Hank's, he was eager to join them. He had a short toboggan for sliding.

The four boys slipped down the path and over the bridge, searching for the best hills.

"There's the beechnut tree!" Louie shouted. "There's a good hill for sliding just on this side of it."

They scrambled down the hill and climbed up the other side of the gully.

"Can I be first? I want to try my new toboggan!" Hank burst out.

Hank sat in the front. Harley climbed on the back.

"Give us a push!" Harley shouted.

Louie gave them a hard shove, and the toboggan picked up speed as it went flying down the hill. The toboggan bounced speedily over the icy crust and downhill bumps. The two boys kept a tight grip on the ropes on each side of the toboggan.

"Watch out!" Hank screamed.

Instantly, the boys hit the dry creek bed at the bottom of the gully.

Hank flew off the front, and Harley landed on top of him.

Louie and Les ran down the hill to where they lay.

They laughed at the two boys rubbing their heads.

"Wow! I forgot about the ditch!" Hank yelled as Harley rubbed his leg.

"We better check the next hill out before we slide," Les said.

The boys pulled their sleds farther toward Spring Creek.

They didn't pass up many hills. Each hill was a challenge to the boys.

"Hey! Look at this hill!" shouted Louie. "It's really steep and looks like fun."

Without thinking, Louie jumped on the Norge tin and started down the hill. The tin lurched as it hit a large bump. It swerved to the left, just missing a small tree. It dipped through the dry creek bed, and Louie almost fell off.

He grabbed the rope on the front of the tin. Louie halted suddenly as he crashed into a bush.

"Boy, you're lucky you didn't run into Big Bear!" shouted Harley. Big Bear was the name of a giant elm tree that stood by itself on the hillside.

After many more slides by everyone, Harley said, "I think we better start heading for home."

As the boys made their way back up the gully toward Hank's house, they took a few more slides.

Harley, Louie, and Les left Hank's and started west across the field toward home. The west wind blew directly into their faces.

"My face is really cold," Les said. "I wish I were home."

"Walk backward for a while," Harley suggested.

So Les and Louie both put their backs to the wind. They stumbled a few times, but it felt better on their faces.

The boys went under the barbed-wire fence where Dad's property began.

They ducked under the fence that led into the little pasture.

"Wow, is my face cold. I think my cheeks are numb!" complained Louie.

Les and Harley put their mittened hands up to their cheeks to check how they felt.

The boys left their sleds under the willow trees and stumbled through the backdoor.

Mum met them at the door. She looked at Les and Louie's faces and said, "Your cheeks are white! I think they're frozen!"

She rubbed her hands against them and exclaimed, "I'll get some damp washcloths for you to hold against your cheeks. They are definitely frozen."

"I can't even feel the cloth," said Louie.

Les also rubbed the damp cloth against his cheeks.

Shortly after, the feeling came back into their cheeks. The boys sat around the table and played a game of Chinese checkers as they thawed out.

Making Metwurst

After the breakfast table was cleared, Dad went to his writing drawer and got some paper.

"I'm going to make a list," he announced.

Louie's head snapped up from the book he was reading. He could tell by Dad's voice that he was planning something interesting.

He peeked over Dad's shoulder as he sat by the kitchen table and wrote:

Pork sausage
Ground beef
Allspice
Casings
Salt
Pepper

"What are you going to make?" asked Louie. "It looks like something good to eat."

"Metwurst!" Dad stated with excitement in his eyes.

"Mm! I can smell it frying already!" Corrine chirped.

"Goodie!" Barbie smiled. "I really like metwurst with pancakes."

Louie's mouth began to water when his sisters talked about the metwurst. He thought of the yummy smell of metwurst smoking in the smokehouse.

Dad told Harley to fetch the sausage-making machine from the basement.

Since it was Saturday—no school and very cold outside—making metwurst sounded like an ideal activity for a day in February.

Dad, Mum, and Virginia placed all the ingredients and supplies on the kitchen counter. Then Mum scrubbed the kitchen table with soapy, warm water. She dried it with a towel.

Dad carefully weighed the sausage and ground beef with a scale placed on the counter. The scale was square with a large, red hand on one side. Dad dumped the meat in the center of the table after it was weighed.

Mum measured the allspice, salt, and pepper with a tablespoon and sprinkled them over the meat.

"Marve, Harley, and Louie, go to the sink and scrub your hands carefully with soap. You must have clean hands," Dad ordered. "You boys may help mix the meat and spices."

After Dad and the three boys had washed their hands, they mixed and squeezed the meat between their fingers. It was cold and greasy. The fatty meat stuck to their hands as they churned and blended the mixture until it was ready to make sausage. Louie thought it was fun to watch the meat as it squeezed between his fingers.

Dad placed the sausage-making machine on one end of the table and then gave instructions.

"Harley and Marve, work the big handle on the machine," ordered Dad. "You may take turns. Make sure you press evenly and slowly down on the handle. Louie, stand over here where the meat mixture enters the casings. I want you to use this small needle to prick the casings if there are air pockets in them."

Casings are pig intestines turned inside out and thoroughly cleaned and soaked in salt water at a meat factory.

"I will guide the sausage as the meat enters the casing," Dad said.

Mum filled the metal container with the meat mixture and placed it on the sausage maker. The container was shaped like a funnel and was gray in color.

Dad took an empty casing and slipped it over the small end of the machine.

Barbie stood on a chair, while Les, Corrine, and Dale sat on chairs near the telephone to watch. Everyone was eager to work or watch the making of metwurst.

"Okay, Marve. Push down slowly on the handle," said Dad.

As Marve pushed, the meat squished out of the machine and into the casings while Dad guided the slippery sausage so it would not break. It looked like Dad was filling a thin balloon with water.

"Here. Prick the casing right here, Louie," Dad instructed. "It might pop if you don't prick the air bubble."

Louie pricked several times. He heard little popping sounds and smelled the allspice that would soon have a smoked aroma.

Virginia held the slippery sausage as Mum tied a strong string on the open end of the sausage so the mixture of meat would stay in the casing. She placed the sausages in a large dishpan, ready for smoking.

Louie looked at the coiled sausages and imagined the crispy, brown sausages on his tongue. He could hardly wait until they were ready to eat.

Later in the afternoon, Mum filled the container for the last time, and Harley pushed down the handle one last time. They were done!

But, they still had some casings left over.

Louie picked up one of the extra casings. He swung it around in a circle. One end of the casing hit Marve's arm.

"Hey! Cut it out!" shouted Marve.

Harley picked up another casing and flipped the loose end and hit Louie in the face.

"Oh, that stinks!" cried Louie.

Les started swinging another casing and flipped it through the air. It slipped out of his hand and wrapped around the telephone speaker that hung on the wall.

Everyone laughed at the casing on the telephone.

"It looks like a dead snake," said Marve, laughing.

The boys kept flipping the casings. They tried to hit each other's faces.

"Phew! What a stink!" said Harley.

Finally, Mum said, "That's enough, boys. You're going to get the curtains dirty."

The boys had fun while it lasted.

Dad tied a binder twine string around each sausage so it could be hung in the smokehouse.

That night, Dad took the dishpan of sausages to the smokehouse, just south of the brooder coop.

Louie followed Dad. He loved the smoky smell of the smokehouse. Sometimes Louie would go alone to the smokehouse, open the door, and breathe in deeply to smell the wonderful aroma of the charred boards.

It smelled delicious.

Dad hung all the metwurst sausages on nails. Nails stuck out on three of the walls and also from the rafter boards that ran from side to side. This gave lots of places to hang the sausages.

"Now let's start a fire," Dad declared.

Dad placed some crumpled paper and dry corncobs in the bottom of a rusty pail. He lit the paper and cobs with a match and gave them time to burn brightly.

Then he placed some corncobs that had been soaking in water on top of the burning cobs. Immediately, the wet cobs began to smolder and smoke. He placed the smoking pail on the ground in the center of the smokehouse below the hanging sausages.

"Now we'll just let it smoke and make good-tasting metwurst," said Dad.

He closed the door, and soon, Louie could see the smoke swirl out of cracks on the side of the smokehouse.

During the next three days, Louie went often to the door of the smokehouse to smell the wonderful aroma.

Dad checked the fire several times a day and added more wet cobs to the smoldering pail.

On the third day, Dad came through the backdoor of the house with a pan full of tasty coils of metwurst.

"Oh, those look so good!" shouted Louie.

He went close to the pan and took a good whiff.

That night, Mum cut a metwurst link in smaller pieces and then split them before she placed them in a frying pan.

The Hooker family enjoyed a mouthwatering meal of homemade bread and metwurst sandwiches for supper.

Louie could hardly wait until Mum would fry metwurst with eggs for breakfast the next morning.

Tin-Can Golf

After the winter snow had melted in the spring of 1948, the Hooker children continually thought of new games to play on the farm.

The boys envied those who could play golf at a golf course. But with such a large family, Louie knew they couldn't afford to play on a beautiful green golf course.

"Why don't we make our own golf course on the farm?" suggested Harley.

Louie piped up, "Yeah, we could use tin cans for holes."

"We could use tennis balls for golf balls," Harley added.

"But what can we use for clubs?" Les chimed in.

"I know," Louie said. "We could use tree limbs shaped like clubs. Our old box elder tree by the backdoor has a lot of good angles on the limbs."

"That sounds like a good idea," responded Harley.

Harley ran to the workshop and grabbed a saw. Then he began climbing the box elder tree. He had to shinny up the tree, because there were no low branches to grab.

"See the limb just below that old robin's nest? It has a nice curve to it!" Louie shouted.

Harley was puffing when he got near the robin's nest.

"You mean this one?" Harley yelled as he pointed.

"Yeah, I want that one," demanded Louie.

Harley began sawing, and Les, who was looking up, began rubbing his eyes.

"I got sawdust in my eyes!" he complained.

The limb dropped to the ground. Louie grabbed it and ran to the workshop for another saw to trim the branch.

When he returned, another branch lay on the ground for Les.

Harley cut two more branches that had good angles.

"There. Now we have an extra one for Marve or Dale if they want to play," Louie added.

The boys finished trimming the branches with the saws. Some of the homemade clubs had big heads. Others had skinny handles. At least they were shaped somewhat like real golf clubs.

The boys hurried to the back of the house and opened the door leading to the basement. On a shelf just before the basement steps, they found a large pail that held tin cans.

They sorted through the cans and found five that seemed the right size— about four inches in diameter. The cans were large enough to leave extra space around a tennis ball so it could easily drop into the can.

They rinsed the cans out with a garden hose behind the house.

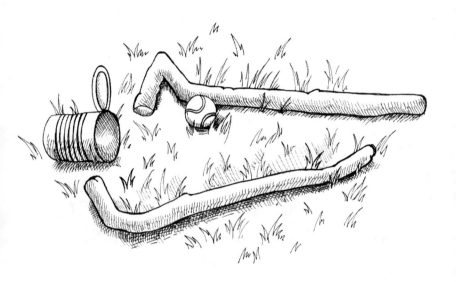

"Louie, will you get a shovel from the shed? Les, help me carry these cans. We'll meet at the pear tree near the sandbox," said Harley.

When they gathered at the pear tree, Harley pointed at the gas pump near the milk house and said, "We'll tee off by the pump for the first hole. Let's put the first can here, near the sandbox.

"Louie, dig a small hole as big as this can," ordered Harley.

As he dug the hole, he hit a big root of the pear tree and had to stomp on the shovel with his foot. He kept glancing at the tin can to make sure the hole was large enough.

Then Harley placed one of the tin cans in the hole. He packed dirt around it and made sure the top of the can was about an inch lower than the dirt around it.

"Now if a ball comes near, it will roll neatly into the can," Harley said.

Then he looked up and asked, "Where should we put the next hole?"

Les looked toward the garden near the apple trees. "Why not put it between those last two clothesline posts near the garden?" asked Les.

The other two boys agreed, so they proceeded to the clothesline posts, and Harley dug and placed hole number two.

"Now where?" Harley asked.

"I think we ought to go way over by the barn," Louie answered.

They all agreed and walked to a spot near the barn.

Louie began digging hole number three and stopped suddenly.

"Look!" he shouted. "See where a mouse made a nest in the tall grass last winter?"

Les grabbed the nest and threw it in the barnyard.

Louie finished digging the hole, and Harley tested rolling a tennis ball into it. It fell into the can easily.

Harley scooped out dirt and placed hole number four near the road north of the driveway.

They used the same hole as number one by the sandbox for the final hole.

The Hooker golf course was completed.

The boys immediately wanted to test the course to see how it worked.

"Les, go to the porch and find three tennis balls in a cardboard box," said

Louie. "I'll get our homemade clubs by the milk house."

The boys gathered at the gas pump.

Harley set his tennis ball on the ground and swung too hard. The ball sailed over the hay rake sitting by the chicken yard fence.

Louie teed off next. He hit the ball on the heel of the club, and it hit the pear tree squarely and bounced back near the little chicken coop.

Les stroked his ball smoothly, and it stopped two feet from the hole.

Harley and Louie each took four strokes to sink their tennis balls in the hole. Les did it in two strokes.

The boys continued on with the course.

When they teed off for hole number three, located near the barn, Les exclaimed, "Let me swing first! I'm the youngest!"

He took a mighty swing, and the tennis ball skimmed past the outhouse and milk house. It landed on the path leading to the barn.

"I'm next!" Louie shouted. He swung with all his might and whiffed it. He missed it completely.

"Aw, shucks!" he muttered.

His next swing put the ball in the sandbox.

Harley was next. His ball whizzed between two clothesline posts and hit the back of the outhouse.

"Well, it looks like Les got the best shot! He always does!" Harley shouted.

The boys thought the course was just perfect. They played many other golf contests throughout the summer.

One time Les completed the small course in twelve strokes. Louie tried desperately to beat his record, but he just couldn't beat Les.

Farm Accidents

Dad made sure no thistles would go to seed in all the pastures throughout the summer. He and his sons would chop them down before the fluffy seeds would fall to the ground and become new thistles.

The boys usually played a game of guessing names of pro baseball players as they hoed the thistles.

One hot, hazy day, while they were hoeing in the little pasture just behind the pigpen, they came upon an extra tall thistle.

Marve said, "I'll get rid of that one. Get out of my way!"

He approached the thistle and took a mighty swing with his hoe. The hoe bounced off the tough stalk of the weed and sliced into his toe. Because the boys often went barefoot, Marve had no protection for his feet.

"Oh, my toe!" yelled Marve. Blood gushed from his big toe.

He fell to the ground, groaning, holding his toe.

Dad checked the cut and said, "We better go to the house and put a tight bandage on it to stop the bleeding."

Marve leaned on Dad's arm as he hobbled toward the house.

Harley and Louie took this opportunity to stop hoeing for a while also. They followed closely behind them and stopped in the entryway.

Louie said, "We better put our shoes on, or we'll chop our toes too."

Mum put salve and a tight bandage on Marve's toe. Then he had to sit in a big chair in the dining room with his foot on a stool.

Dad, Harley, and Louie went back to the pasture to finish hoeing.

The two boys chopped with extra care. They soon finished, and Dad said, "There. Now all the thistles we hoed will not go to seed, and the cows will have a better pasture next year."

The next week, another accident happened on the farm.

Dad often let a young bull graze on the tall grass growing just north of the driveway.

He placed a stake in the ground with a long rope fastened to a collar around the bull's neck. This gave the bull a large circle of grass to eat.

One morning, Dad drove the tractor with the trailer behind down the driveway near where the bull was staked.

Louie happened to be near the bull as Dad drove by.

"Watch out! Don't let the bull get you!" Dad yelled, jokingly.

Louie thought Dad meant it seriously and began to back away from the bull.

Thud! One of the trailer wheels ran over Louie's foot.

He lay on the ground near the bull, groaning and rubbing his ankle.

Dad jumped off the tractor and looked at Louie's ankle. It was beginning to swell.

Dad shook his head with regret and said, "I'm sorry, Louie. I shouldn't have scared you."

Louie was too easily fooled. He limped to the house, leaning on Dad. Mum put ice on his ankle and told him to sit quietly in the dining room.

Later the following week, Les, Dale, and Louie were peeking into the swallow nests on the front porch. The birds had smeared mud near the top of the porch posts, making sturdy nests for their babies. Swallows darted around their heads like out-of-control arrows.

"Look at that one!" Dale said. "I can see five heads sticking over the edge of the nest."

Les and Louie turned their heads upward to glance at the tiny beaks above the rim of the nest.

Just then, the boys heard a tap on the big window beside them. They turned and saw Barbie leaning over the back of the large rocking chair and peering out at them.

Dale rushed to the window.

"Look at the tiny swallows in the nest on the corner!" he yelled, pointing.

Barbie leaned over to look upward.

Suddenly, the rocking chair tipped over backward. Barbie and the back of the rocking chair crashed through the window. Glass flew in all directions. As Dale tried to catch Barbie, a jagged piece of glass hit his arm and pierced his skin.

"Oh, I got cut!" yelled Dale.

Blood began dripping on the porch floor.

Barbie lay sprawled on the porch near where Dale was standing. She had a very surprised look on her face. She had a cut on her arm too.

Dale ran to the front door of the house, holding his bleeding arm with his hand.

Mum met him at the door. She quickly wrapped his arm with a clean cloth to stop the bleeding.

Mum then rushed to Barbie, who was still standing perplexed on the porch.

"Come quickly!" she shouted to Barbie. "I'll take care of your cut."

The next day, Dad had a glass man from Fremont replace the large window with new glass.

Dad's Singing

The corn grew fast that summer, and so did the weeds.

Dad surely enjoyed his John Deere tractor. He loved using it for cultivating the corn. The cultivator shovels did a good job of ripping out the weeds around the corn.

The *putt-putt-putt* of the tractor echoed from the cornfield west of the road.

Louie sat on the steps of the front porch. A swallow darted near his head. The swallow had a nest made of mud near the corner post. Louie could hear the young swallows chirp as their mother brought them some bugs for breakfast.

Louie watched Dad as he looked steadily down the rows of corn. The tractor needed to go straight and true, so no corn was dug from the ground by the cultivators.

Then Louie heard a sound above the steady noise of the tractor. Dad was singing:

O beautiful for spacious skies,
For amber waves of grain,
For purple mountain majesties
Above the fruited plain!
America! America!
God shed his grace on thee,
And crown Thy good
with brotherhood
From sea to shining sea!

Dad loved to sing as he cultivated. Many neighbors said they heard and enjoyed his singing.

Louie was glad his dad sang and enjoyed life.

Louie began to sing:

O beautiful for spacious skies,
For amber waves of grain.

Brownie came from under the box elder tree and sat beside him. He wagged his tail and put his head on Louie's knee as Louie gently and lovingly patted his head.

Dad kept singing, and Louie and Brownie sat on the steps and listened.

Dad came to the end of the row at the road and turned the tractor around.

Once again, he sang:

On a hill far away
Stood an old rugged cross,
The emblem of suff'ring
and shame;
And I love that old cross
Where the dearest and best
For a world of lost
sinners was slain.
So I'll cherish the old
rugged cross,
Till my trophies at
last I lay down;
I will cling to the old
rugged cross,
And exchange it someday
for a crown.

As Louie scratched Brownie's ear, he thought of the Fourth of July celebration coming next week.

His head nodded. He lay down on the porch and fell asleep, with Brownie lying beside him.

The Fourth of July

Dad drove to Bill Tanises' welding shop. The cutting blade on his haymower needed welding.

"Hi, Reen. Are you remembering tomorrow is the Fourth of July?" Bill questioned.

"Yeah, we have a few firecrackers," Dad answered.

Louie nudged Dad. He remembered Bill had given them some carbide the year before.

Dad got the hint.

"You wouldn't have some carbide to spare, would you?"

Bill chuckled and gave a nod to show he would give them some. Bill's sister was married to Dad's oldest brother, Rens.

Bill found an empty can and dumped some of the carbide powder into it. He used carbide for welding.

Louie knew it could also be used for fun on the Fourth of July.

"Louie, remember to let Harley and Marve help you use this tomorrow," Dad warned.

The next morning began with a glorious sunrise in the east. Before Louie arose from bed, he thought of all the exciting events of the day: good food, firecrackers, a carnival at White Cloud, and fireworks.

It was Louie's turn to get the cows for milking. He lay in the straw with Brownie and Blackie as Dad changed the milking machines. He was eager to use the carbide with his older brothers after breakfast.

All the boys hastened out the backdoor as soon as Dad finished the morning devotions at the table.

They hustled to the backdoor of the milk house. Marve picked up the can of carbide, and Harley grabbed the old paint can next to it. Louie, Les, and Dale were waiting impatiently at the sidewalk near the windmill.

"Louie, run to the house and get a box of matches!" Marve yelled.

When he returned with the matches, the boys gathered around the paint can that Marve placed on the sidewalk.

"Harley, put about two spoons of carbide in the bottom of the paint can!" ordered Marve.

"Okay," Harley responded as he proceeded to spoon the powder into the can.

Then Marve poured a little water from a small bottle into the can with the powder. He stirred it with a stick to form a pasty substance. A gas began rising from the can. He quickly replaced the cover.

Harley stomped on the can cover with his foot to shut it tightly.

Louie smelled the gas created when the water was mixed with carbide powder.

The bottom of the paint can had a very small hole made by pounding a nail into it.

"Get back now!" Marve warned.

Harley lit a match. He held it next to the little hole at the bottom of the paint can.

Kaboom! The cover flew off the can.

When a match is held at the hole, the gas made by mixing carbide and water creates an explosion.

Throughout the day, the boys set off many more carbide cans. They also lit some firecrackers.

Louie put cotton in his ears so the noise would not hurt them.

After the evening chores, the family climbed in the blue Dodge and headed for White Cloud.

Everyone expected to see the fireworks and go on some carnival rides.

After turning the corner at Reeman Church on Seventy-Second Street, Les shouted, "What are all those people doing in Penny Tanises' hayfield?"

As they approached Penny's farm, Louie yelled, "They're playing ball!"

Penny was given this nickname because he swallowed a penny when he was a young boy.

Dad suggested, "Should we stop and join them?"

Harley, Louie, and Les quickly responded, "Yes!"

They were always ready for a softball game.

When Dad turned the corner and drove into the Tanises' driveway, they saw a large group of Penny's brothers' and sisters' families.

Penny approached and asked, "Do you want to play ball?"

"Yes!" the boys shouted.

"Okay, let's stay," Dad said.

The Hooker family piled out of the car. The boys and Dad divided up so some were on each team.

The hay had been cut and put in the barn the week before. This gave plenty of space to play ball in the hayfield. They used bags for bases. The bags were made from a coarse, brown material called burlap.

When Harley came up to bat, he hit the ball far out to Seventy-Second Street. He ran all the way to third base. Les was the next batter and hit the ball far out to right field and ran safely to second base.

Later, when it was Louie's turn to bat, he wanted so much to show what a good batter he was. He swung with all his might. He missed the ball completely. On the next pitch, Louie thought, *I've got to keep my eye on the ball*. Once again, he gave a strong swing at the ball. It dribbled slowly to the first baseman, Neil, Penny's brother. Louie was out. He was very disappointed with his performance.

When it got too dark to play ball, Penny hollered, "Let's stop and have some fireworks!"

With the help of some of the men, Penny lit large Roman candles and other bright and colorful fireworks some distance from the crowd of people.

Dad said, "These fireworks are just as brilliant as the ones in White Cloud. We didn't have to go a long way to see them either."

After an exciting night of *oohs* and *ahs*, the Hookers said good-bye to the Tanis family and thanked them for a fun time.

Another Fourth of July had ended, and America was 172 years old.

Pet Crows

Louie lay in his bed near a window upstairs. The window was open, and he moved his head close to the screen. He heard the caw of a crow way off in the distance. Another crow answered nearby.

This reminded Louie of what Cousin Hank had said a few days earlier: "Wouldn't it be fun to get some baby crows and train them to talk?"

Farmers didn't like crows because they destroyed corn and other crops.

Louie planned to do something about Hank's suggestion. He jumped out of bed, slipped his clothes on; and ran downstairs.

"Shall we get crows today?" he asked Harley, who was sitting at the kitchen table.

"Yeah," Harley answered, remembering what Hank had said the week before.

Les, sitting at the table next to Harley, cried, "I want to go too!"

Louie asked Dad, who came through the door, "Can we go to the gully with Hank today?"

"Well," Dad answered, "we're pretty well caught up with the farm work, so I think that will be okay."

"Yippee!" the boys chorused together.

The three boys got their fishing poles ready and made sure all their lines had good hooks. They might as well go fishing too.

Harley found a sturdy cardboard box in the basement.

Then Mum came out the backdoor of the house and yelled, "You boys get some hoes and help me clean the garden first! The weeds are getting out of control and need hoeing today!"

"Aw, do we have to?" Louie complained.

"Yes, you know you like to eat the strawberries as well as anyone. So let's get to work," Mum replied.

Louie went to the shed where the hoes stood in a corner and brought them to the garden.

Harley and Les strolled up to where Louie and Mum were standing.

"I want each of you to start on a row of the strawberries that we planted in April," suggested Mum. "Be careful. Don't hoe out the plants, and make sure you get all the weeds."

The boys each started on the strawberries, and Mum worked on some rows of sweet corn.

When they had something to look forward to, the boys did a good job of staying on task.

"I hope we find four little crows so we can each have one," Les said, working with a short hoe that he could handle.

"Yeah," Louie said. "We can put them in the gopher cage so they don't get killed by the cats."

"Oops! I cut off a plant!" Louie yelled.

"You be careful!" Mum shouted.

The boys finished their job in good time, but Mum told them they had to wait until after dinner to walk across the field to Hank's.

While they were waiting for noon and dinner, the boys got a tin can and dug some worms for fishing. They found some big, juicy worms in a wet spot under the apple trees in the garden.

At noon, they hurriedly downed their dinner and headed for Hank's.

Les carried the worms in a fish pail, Louie carried the fishing poles, and Harley carried the cardboard box for the crows.

Hank saw them coming and met them on the road in front of his house.

"What's that box for?" he asked Harley.

"Maybe we can get those baby crows today," he answered.

"That sounds like fun!" cried Hank.

Hank grabbed his fishing pole, and the four boys walked down into the gully behind the barn. Since it was summer and it hadn't rained for some time, the creek was dry.

"Did you hear that?" Louie asked.

"No," the other three boys chorused.

"What did you hear?" asked Harley.

"I think I heard a baby crow make a cawing sound," Louie answered.

Everyone stopped walking and stood quietly. They hoped to hear it again.

"Caw! Caw!" A very distinct sound of a baby crow sounded from the east.

They listened again. They could hear two caws at nearly the same time.

"There must be more than one!" yelled Hank. "They're probably in a nest high in a tree!"

"Listen," Harley said. "We have to walk quietly and not talk. We don't want the mother crow to hear us, and we want the babies to keep cawing."

The four boys stepped softly through the tall grasses in a single file. Harley and Hank took turns leading the group as Louie and Les followed. They walked in a crouched position, thinking it was a sneakier and quieter way to approach the nest.

Les stumbled over an anthill and fell on his hands to the ground. Louie gave him a dirty look and reminded him to use his best sneak methods.

Each time the boys heard a crow caw, they sped up and walked more quickly.

As they approached the point where Spring Creek from the north met the dry creek bed from the west, the cawing became louder. It was coming from the gully toward Gerrit Sneller's farm.

Hank motioned to the other three to crouch lower and whispered, "Walk very softly. Keep low. We want the babies to keep cawing so we can find their tree."

A huge pine tree stood on the west bank of the gully. Les pointed at the tree after an exceptionally loud caw.

"The crows' nest is in that tree," he whispered.

Now the boys could run. They knew where the nest was. Harley reached the tree first and pointed at a dark wad of sticks and leaves about twenty feet from the ground.

"I see a baby crow's head sticking over the edge of the nest!" shouted Louie.

The four boys advanced toward the pine tree. Brambles surrounded the tree, and many prickers stuck on their shirts.

Harley and Hank led the way into the sharp needles of the pine tree. They quietly began climbing the tree so the baby crows would remain in the nest. The sticky sap of the tree coated their hands and clothes.

The mother crow cawed loudly from the top of an oak tree to the east. The babies were quiet; they understood their mother's warning caw.

The two older boys were getting near the nest. Louie and Les stayed on the lower branches.

They watched Harley grab a baby crow. Hank quickly took a second one. A third one jumped out of the nest and tumbled to the lower branches. It squawked as it landed with a thump right near where Louie was sitting on a branch. Louie stuck out his hand and grabbed the crow by its legs.

"Are there any more?" Les shouted.

"Nope," Harley answered. "There were just three."

"Aw, shucks!" Les cried. "I wanted to have one for a pet too!"

"You can help me with mine," Louie said. "Ouch! He just scratched me!"

The boys carefully climbed down from the prickly branches of the pine tree.

They all sat down on the grassy slope of the gully. Les sat beside Louie and stroked the back of the baby bird as Louie held tightly onto its legs. The baby crows fluttered their wings to show they didn't like being prisoners.

"Well, Les, you carry all our fishing poles. We'll carry the rest of the fishing stuff," Harley said.

Les gave a sigh of discontent because there was no baby crow for him.

The four boys forgot about fishing. They had some new pets to tend.

When they arrived at Hank's place, Harley and Louie decided not to use the box. Instead, they carried their new pets in their arms. They couldn't wait to show their brothers and sisters.

Harley, Louie, and Les walked across the field to their home. The two baby crows squawked and flapped their wings occasionally, trying to escape. Louie fell once and lost hold of his crow. It fluttered its wings, desperately trying to escape captivity, but the boys cornered it near the fence post where a bluebird had a nest. The baby bluebirds chirped when they heard the boys talking.

The boys proceeded home, past the pigpen, to the little chicken coop.

"Here, Les. You hold my crow while I get the cage out of the workshop," Harley ordered.

Les was eager to hold the baby crow.

Soon Harley appeared with the cage that had held many other Hooker pets, like muskrats, rabbits, gophers, snakes, and opossums.

They stuffed their two pet crows through the door on the top.

"Let's get the chores done," Harley said. "The neighbor boys are coming over to play softball tonight."

With no time to play with the crows, Louie and his brothers had to wait until morning to begin training the crows.

A Dead Crow

That night, Louie lay awake, thinking of all the ways he could train his crow. He remembered Hank had said that you could even teach a crow to talk. But you had to split their tongue so they could do it.

Louie thought it would be too hard because they didn't have a doctor around to operate on the crows' tongues.

Louie awakened early the next morning. He glanced over toward Harley's bed. He saw him turn over and thought he was about to awaken.

"Harley, are you awake?"

"Huh, why? Is something wrong?"

"No, but do you want to see how our crows are doing?"

"Oh, I guess so, but I feel pretty sleepy yet."

The boys slipped into their clothes and went down the stairway.

Mum was just coming out of her bedroom.

"Why are you boys awake so early?"

"We're gonna check on our crows," Louie answered. "I hope the cats didn't get them."

The screen door slammed behind Louie as he rushed toward the cage under the little willow tree. Harley was right behind him. Huddled together in one corner of the cage, the crows cawed as they saw the boys approach them.

"Are you hungry?" shouted Louie.

One of the crows cawed softly, as if to answer "yes."

Louie ran into the house and got a crust of bread and some milk in a glass. He dipped a piece of the crust into the milk and set it on a board. He then placed it in front of the crows inside the cage.

Both crows cocked their heads and peered at the soggy bread. Neither of them ate it.

Harley opened the cage door again and took his crow out of the cage. He could tell it was his because it was larger than Louie's crow. Harley's crow fluttered its wings some but then sat quietly on his knee. Harley dipped some crust into the milk.

"Louie, pry open its beak," he said.

Louie cautiously grabbed its beak, thinking the crow might peck him. As soon as its beak opened, Harley stuffed the wet bread into the crow's mouth. With some coughing, the crow swallowed the bread.

The next crust went down the crow's throat more smoothly. After a short time, the crow opened its beak without Louie's help.

Then the boys fed Louie's crow in the same manner.

The next day, the crows ate raw hamburger out of the boys' hands.

By the next week, Harley and Louie could let the crows sit on their laps without holding their legs.

Louie named his crow Blackie, and Harley named his Coal.

Later one morning, Louie fed Blackie some dry breadcrumbs. Blackie was very hungry and cawing for more.

Suddenly, Blackie pooped all over Louie's bare leg. Louie was wearing shorts, and the slimy poop ran down his leg.

"Oh, Les, run and get an old towel to clean my leg off!" Louie yelled.

"Blackie, you're going back in your cage if you're going to be so messy!" cried Louie.

After Louie cleaned up the mess on his leg, the boys sat and watched Blackie and Coal hop around in their cage.

Louie wondered if they would ever teach the crows any good tricks. It seemed like all they wanted to do was eat.

The next week, Harley and Louie walked across the field to Hank's place again. Harley brought Dad's old twelve-gauge shotgun.

When they arrived, Hank had his sixteen-gauge shotgun ready. He met the two boys at the road.

Hank told Harley, "Other crows are trying to lure my pet crow back into the woods. They want my pet crow to become a wild crow again."

"Those crows are right behind the barn now!" shouted Hank. "Let's sneak around the north side of the barn and surprise them."

Louie followed behind the two boys who had guns.

"Don't make a sound as we sneak around the barn," Hank warned.

The three boys crawled on their stomachs just beside the lane that went down into the gully. They were determined to stop those wild crows from kidnapping Hank's pet.

As they neared the corner of the barn, Hank peeked around the corner. Harley was by his side, and Louie was two steps behind them.

The two crows sat on a woodpile, cawing with all their might, calling to Hank's crow to come join them.

Harley whispered to Hank, "You shoot the closest one, and I'll shoot the farthest one."

"Okay!" Hank whispered. "On the count of three. One. Two. Three."

Bang! Bang!

The closer crow flew away. The farther one keeled over backward, appearing to be dead.

The boys rushed quickly to the woodpile, where the two crows had been sitting.

The sun gleamed on the shiny black neck feathers of the crumpled crow.

Hank picked up the dead crow and examined it.

"Harley!" Hank shouted. "I think you shot my pet crow! I thought he was by the house, but he was out here!"

The three boys sat on the woodpile, looking sadly at the dead crow.

"Well," Hank remarked, "I guess those wild crows won't kidnap my pet anymore."

Harley and Louie agreed as the three boys walked slowly toward the shed to find a shovel to bury the pet.

Within the next few weeks, both Blackie and Coal died in their cage the same night. The boys never knew what caused it, but Dad said they probably got some virus.

While it lasted, the crow pets had been fun, but Louie said to Harley and Les, "I think dogs are a lot easier to train."

The Lost Puppy

Louie eagerly pedaled his blue bike with all his might south down Fitzgerald Avenue.

Les raced closely behind on his Billy Boy bike, a smaller bike than Louie's.

"Oops! The fishing poles came loose!" yelled Louie.

The boys stopped and untangled the strings on their crude fishing poles made from the limbs of a box elder tree.

Louie looked with pride at his bike as he carefully tied the poles to its frame. It was a girl's bike. Dad had bought it from Margaret DeVries, the minister's daughter.

Blackie and Brownie, the family pups, ran closely behind the bikes as they sped toward Spring Creek.

Brownie yipped when he fell behind, so the boys stopped briefly to let him catch up.

White, puffy clouds drifted across the blue sky.

Louie moved his feet faster on the pedals as a striped gopher scampered across the road in front of him. Tall grass was waving with the breeze on either side of Eightieth Street.

The boys approached the dump just before the dip in the road.

"Let's find some Prince Albert tobacco cans before we go fishing," Louie hollered as Les braked his bike to a halt.

They stepped carefully through the glass bottles and cans of the dump.

"It's a good thing we wore our shoes!" Les yelled. "There is a lot of broken glass!"

"Look, Les. I found a nice clean Prince Albert can."

"Here's another one," Les answered.

The boys stuck them in the pockets of their bib overalls.

"We can put wheat in them when we get home," Louie suggested. "Then we can chew the wheat like chewing tobacco."

The two of them hopped on their bikes and braked down the hill to the bridge below.

"Let's hide our bikes behind this bush," said Louie.

Blackie and Brownie sniffed at a place where a rabbit had left some fur on a burdock weed.

Les ran down to the creek and started looking for fishing holes. The boys followed the creek through the purple-headed thistles and brown dock weeds.

The dogs ran ahead and stopped at a sandy spot near the creek.

Brownie abruptly jumped backward as a big green bullfrog dove into the creek in front of him.

He watched it swim across the creek as he peeked over the bank to gaze at it.

Ker splash! Brownie lost his balance and plunged under the water.

"Look at crazy Brownie!" shouted Louie, as Les looked up from a spot down the creek where he was fishing.

Brownie's head stayed above water as he dog-paddled to the other shore. He struggled up the sandy bank and shook the water from his soaked body.

"He sure looks goofy, all wet and soggy," Les said, laughing.

Soon the boys began to fish intently. They caught six sheep fish, eight shiners, and five horned aces. Les even caught a little sucker.

When they approached the old swimming hole, the boys began to quicken their step. Louie imagined the many fish waiting to be caught as he ran ahead and stared at the huge hole. Right in the center of the hole floated what looked like an enormous round piece of wood.

Louie ran closer.

"Wow! Look at the size of that snapping turtle!" he screamed. It was bigger than Louie's chest.

"Boy, I'd like to catch him on my fishing pole!" Les yelled. The two pups ran near the creek.

"Oh, there goes the turtle underwater!" Louie yelled.

"Well, I guess I'm not going swimming today," Les said. "I'm afraid the turtle will grab my toe."

"Me neither!" said Louie, laughing.

The boys caught fifteen more fish from the old swimming hole throughout the afternoon. They placed them in the fish pail to save for the barn tank.

"Well, I think it's about time to get our bikes and head for home," said Louie when the fishing slacked off.

Les agreed and whistled for the pups. Brownie approached from behind a big tree.

Louie whistled and yelled, "Here, Blackie! Here, Blackie!"

Blackie didn't appear.

The boys laid their fishing gear down in the grass and began to hunt. They scoured both sides of the creek and up and down the gully.

They kept calling, "Here, Blackie! Here, Blackie!" They whistled many times.

No Blackie.

After an hour or so, Louie said, "We better go home, or they'll worry about us."

So the boys, with Brownie, followed the creek back to their bikes.

Les tied the poles on his bike, and Louie carried the fish pail on his handlebars.

As they turned from the road into the driveway, the boys met Dad walking from the barn.

"Where's Blackie?" he questioned.

"We lost him," Louie responded with a troubled look on his face.

"How did that happen?" asked Dad.

"When we finished fishing, we whistled and called, and he didn't come!" Louie responded.

"Well, we better eat supper, and then Harley can drive you over there to see if you can find him," Dad added.

The boys emptied their fish in the barn tank. There were thirty-five all together.

Brownie followed the boys to the house. He whimpered as if to tell them he missed his brother.

Louie and Les ate their supper anxiously. Then they hurried with Harley to the 1935 black Ford. The floorboards had holes in them, and dust rolled up through the cracks as they sped toward the gully and Spring Creek.

Harley parked the car on the side of the road near the dump. The boys jumped out of the car and scampered down the hill to the bridge. They called, "Here, Blackie! Here, Blackie!"

They waited. There was no response. No Blackie.

"Remember, Les, we crossed the creek on a log. Maybe Blackie stayed on the other side of the creek," Louie suggested.

"Yeah, I remember," Les answered.

"Well, let's drive the car over on Brucker Avenue," Harley said. "Then we can walk toward the creek from that direction."

So the three boys walked back up the hill. They continued to call for Blackie.

Harley drove the Ford through the dip in the road and onto Brucker from Eightieth Street.

Two horses grazed in the field to the west of the road. They looked up as Harley parked the car and the boys piled out.

"Here, Blackie! Here, Blackie!" the three boys chorused.

"Come on, boy!" yelled Louie. "Here's some foodie food!"

No puppy appeared.

The boys walked down a small ravine that led into the gully and Spring Creek, calling as they walked.

Finally, Louie yelled, "I see a black spot moving in some thistles ahead!"

"Here, Blackie!" The black spot burst from the thistles and into Louie's arms. Blackie's whole body was wiggling like Jell-O.

Many burrs hung from his black coat, but he was safe.

Les and Harley hustled to Louie and Blackie. The pup licked their faces in greeting.

This time, Blackie tagged along closely behind the boys as they walked back to the car. He didn't stop to sniff at any gopher holes. He wanted to go home.

The rest of the Hooker family gave Blackie a warm greeting at the big white house. Blackie also gave each of them a lick on the face.

Brownie came barking from the barn to investigate what was happening. When he saw Blackie, he whimpered joyfully and happily licked his brother's face.

The two puppies slept together again in the barn alleyway that night.

The Lost Girl

Les, Barbie, and Louie were on the front lawn playing with a little red wagon. Blackie was barking happily as he ran beside them. Blackie liked playing with the children much more than his twin brother, Brownie. He nipped at their heels and yapped with every step he took. A passing butterfly drew his attention. Then he bounced toward the cedar tree as he chased the flitting butterfly.

Barbie yelled to the boys, "Hey, will you give me a ride in the wagon? Louie, you pull, and Les, you push!"

"Okay," the boys answered. They began wheeling Barbie across the brown summer grass. They went toward the garden and then in between the cedar trees near the road.

Thunk!

"What was that?" questioned Louie.

They looked toward the dusty gravel road. A big black car left a cloud of dust as it went south down the road.

When the dust settled, Les screamed, "Oh no!"

They could see a little black object lying on the side of the road. Louie and Les ran through the ditch. Barbie tore to the big white house as fast as her little legs could take her.

When Louie and Les got to the road, they found Blackie. He lay in a little heap, still and frightening.

"I think we better take him up by the barn," Louie said. "He's dead!"

He picked him up carefully, placed him in the red wagon, and pulled it slowly toward the barn. Les followed quietly behind. Some tears were in both of their eyes.

When they got to the barn, Dad was doing chores.

Louie called from the barn door, "Dad, look what happened to Blackie."

As Dad approached, he said, "I knew this was going to happen one of these days. Blackie never watched for cars when he was near the road. Let me finish these chores. We'll bury him by the power pole."

Dad hurried to finish the chores. Louie and Les watched him dig a hole. They carefully placed Blackie in the hole and filled it with brown sand.

"Let's go to the house for supper," Dad said. They could smell Mum's chicken pie as they neared the house. They washed their hands, and everyone sat down to eat—everyone except Barbie.

"Where's Barbie?" Mum asked.

"She was playing on the front lawn with us," Les said. "When Blackie got hit by the car, we didn't see her anymore."

"We better find her," Dad said.

Everyone got up from the table to hunt. Dad, Marve, Harley, and Dale ran outside to look.

Dad yelled, "Barbie, where are you?"

There was no answer.

They searched behind the bushes in the front yard. They looked in the milk house and in many of the other buildings.

While they were hunting outside, Mum, Virginia, Louie, Les, and Corrine looked for Barbie inside the house.

"Barbie, can you hear me?" Mum shouted.

Barbie did not answer.

They looked closely inside her bedroom upstairs. They checked behind the old chest in the attic and behind the curtain that was drawn by the window. They couldn't find her anywhere.

"Let's go downstairs to look," Mum said with a worried look on her face. They looked everywhere in the living room. They searched the little kitchen and the back porch.

No Barbie.

Just as the others came from outside, Mum yelled from the spare bedroom, "I found her. She's in the closet in the dark."

Everyone ran to the spare bedroom.

Barbie came slowly out of the closet, her face red and blotchy. Tears were running down her cheeks.

"I…I…I was so sad when Blackie got hit. I ran to the closet to cry by myself."

Mum put her arm around Barbie and wiped her face with her apron. "Let's go eat some chicken pie," she said comfortingly to Barbie.

Everyone sat down quietly with sad thoughts. Dad said a prayer, and everyone ate their chicken pie.

For some time after, life on the Hooker farm seemed sad without the sound of Blackie yipping, but the lost girl had been found.

Farm Chores

Louie and his brothers didn't play all the time. They had chores and many kinds of work on the farm.

Marve, Harley, and Louie often wheeled cow manure from the gutter to a manure pile in the barnyard.

One Saturday morning, Dad suggested, "I think you boys should move the planks on the pile of manure. It's getting too high to push the wheelbarrow to the top."

It took a lot of strength to push a wheelbarrow with a full load of manure on a plank eight inches wide up a steep incline.

"Marve, it's too cold to fuss around this morning outside on top of the manure pile. Let's wait a couple of days," whined Louie.

Marve agreed to wait.

After breakfast the next day, Louie went to the barn to clean out the gutters. A gutter is a trench made of cement located behind the cattle. It caught the manure from the cows where they stood in their stalls.

Louie used the big scoop fork to shovel the manure from the gutter into the wheelbarrow. He made the load extra large so he could finish the gutter on the south end. The slimy heap of cow flops rounded up above the wheelbarrow. It reached as high as Louie's chest.

"Do you want me to take it out?" Marve offered.

"No, I filled it, so I'll unload it!" Louie snapped.

Louie sighed heavily, opened the east barn door, and lifted the handles. He wheeled it down the ramp from the barn. It wobbled back and forth because the load was so huge.

Louie was determined to make it to the manure pile. The horrid stink filled his nostrils as he trudged along the wooden planks.

Louie's heart beat faster when his foot slipped as he went up the incline to the pile. His arms were growing weary.

The wheelbarrow tipped to the side. Louie struggled to steady the load but instead plunged his hand into the juicy poop.

"Oh, yuck!" Louie moaned. "My hand is covered with poop!"

Marve came quickly to dump the load. Louie ran to the barn tank and cleaned his hands.

"I guess we should have listened to Dad," Louie whimpered as he shook his hands dry in the air. "Let's move the boards to another spot so we don't have such a steep hill."

"Okay," Marve said.

Together, they moved the planks to be ready for the next gutter cleaning.

On the following Saturday, Dad suggested, "Harley, Louie, and Les, I would like you boys to clean the chicken roosts in the big and little chicken coops this morning."

"Okay," the boys echoed.

They were eager to listen to the Michigan-Michigan State football game on the radio at noon. They hurried to get started.

Les and Louie grabbed the tub from the cooker room. It was named the cooker room because it contained a large iron pot where water was boiled for butchering hogs.

Harley got a long scraper from the tool shed.

They used the scraper to pull the chicken droppings from the roosts.

As the boys walked into the coop, the chickens cackled. It disturbed them from eating their breakfast of chicken mash. Mash is corn, wheat, and oats ground up and mixed together.

Harley used a two-foot-long stick to prop up the first roost. The roost was made from chicken wire on a wooden frame. The wood frame had hinges in the back so the front could be lifted.

The chicken droppings fell through the wire holes and kept the roost clean where the chickens' feet rested.

Louie grabbed the scraper and pulled the droppings from the back to the front of the roost. As the droppings tumbled over the edge, they dribbled into a waiting tub.

Les kept moving the tub as Louie kept pulling the chicken manure from the roost.

"The tub's full!" Les exclaimed.

Harley grabbed one handle of the tub; Louie grabbed the other. They carried the full tub through the door as Les held it open.

The boys dumped the tub of chicken manure into a manure spreader parked near the door.

When they returned to the coop, they found Les playing with a rooster. He would fake that he was scared of it. The rooster would boldly chase him until Les turned around abruptly. The rooster would bump into him and then scurry away. He found out that Les wasn't scared after all.

After the boys finished cleaning out both the big and little coops, Dad had enough manure in the spreader to fertilize a large patch in next year's cornfield.

The boys also finished in time to listen to the football game on the radio.

Driving Tractors

Louie lay in bed, thinking about the next day. He also recalled the first time he had driven Dad's John Deere H tractor. This is how it happened.

The place was just off the lane to the fields west of the road.

Dad asked Louie if he would like to drive the tractor home.

Louie responded with an enthusiastic "yes!"

He was always jealous of Harley, who knew so much about driving the tractor.

Louie jumped eagerly onto the seat of the tractor. He had watched Harley and Dad many times as he sat on the fender of the tractor.

He pushed the clutch lever with a confident hand. The tractor with trailer behind lurched forward and to the left. Louie grabbed the steering wheel quickly and steered it to the right. The tractor swerved too far to the right, so Louie turned it nervously to the left again.

He continued over-steering to the right and then to the left several times until Dad yelled, "Pull the clutch lever!"

Louie grabbed the lever and pulled backward with all his might. The tractor and trailer jolted to a sudden stop. Les and Harley, who sat in the trailer, rubbed their sore necks from the sudden halt.

Louie felt embarrassed. He failed his first attempt at driving a tractor. The tongue of the trailer was rubbing against the back tire of the tractor. The tractor and trailer sat in a crooked position.

After Louie got off the tractor, Harley hopped onto the seat and drove it down the lane to the shed.

After that, Louie drove many other times as Dad used the tractor for other farm chores. He learned not to over-steer the tractor and to move the steering wheel only a short distance each time to the left or right.

Tomorrow, the neighborhood men were coming to fill the silo, and Louie would be driving many tractors.

Louie slowly drifted off to sleep.

"Harley, Louie, Les, and Dale, time to get up if you want to watch silo filling today." Mum was standing at the bottom of the stairway.

Louie popped up, quickly slipped his clothes on, and rushed down the stairway. His brothers followed right behind him.

Dad sat at the kitchen table. He offered a prayer and asked God to bless their day of filling silo. After a hasty breakfast, Dad, Louie, and Harley hurried outside to feed and water the chickens. Louie carried pails of water from the milk house and dumped them into large pans in the chicken coops. The chickens cackled and pecked at the corn that Dad had thrown in spots on the floor.

After chores the men began to arrive with their tractors and wagons.

Just as Louie stepped out of the chicken coop door, he heard the roar of the first tractor arriving. It was Ed Tanis with his Minneapolis Moline tractor.

Gerrit Sneller, on his Ford, and Penny Tanis, on his Ferguson, parked their tractors near the barn. Uncle Garrit Hooker came slowly up the driveway on a John Deere H the same time Gerrit Boes turned in with his John Deere A.

Louie stood on the cement walk and watched each of these men arrive. Then he slowly turned his eyes up the road to the north. He heard the chug of a different kind of tractor. Then he saw him—Harry Tanis on his Doodlebug.

Louie's heart thumped. This was a different kind of tractor, and he was eager to drive it. The Doodlebug was an old Model A Ford car that had been changed so that it was stronger and could pull a heavy load of corn.

Louie hoped he could drive the Doodlebug today. He and Harley expected to drive all the different kinds of tractors. The Doodlebug was exciting; it was almost like driving a car.

"Hi, Louie!" Penny Tanis yelled. "Do you want to drive my tractor today?"

"Yeah!" Louie answered. "That will be fun!"

On the day before, Dad had used a corn binder to cut and bind the stalks of corn. The binder bound several stalks together with a heavy string called twine. Many bundles of corn now lay throughout the field.

By 9:30 Saturday morning, the men were ready to start loading the bundles of corn onto wagons. This is what Louie was waiting for. He jumped on Gerrit Sneller's Ford tractor as soon as Gerrit arrived in the corn field.

The Ford had a foot clutch, like a car. When you put it in gear and lifted your foot, it moved.

Louie was more familiar with a hand clutch, or lever, because Dad's John Deere H had one. Louie liked the Ford because it was different.

With Harley and Louie driving their tractors, the men could lay the bundles of corn on the wagons without getting on and off their tractors.

Since Harley had beat Louie to the Doodlebug, Louie had to wait his turn.

Louie rode on Gerrit Sneller's corn wagon to the barn and silo. He wanted to watch the start of filling the silo at the barn.

Ed Tanis used his yellow Minneapolis Moline tractor to turn a long belt. The belt ran to the silo filler. Ed shouted, "Are you ready to start?"

"Okay," Dad answered. "Let her go!"

The yellow tractor roared, and the belt slowly moved and began to whir.

Louie and Les stood by the corner of the barn, watching the men intently.

Dad and Ed Tanis placed stalks of corn on the table of the filler, bottom end first. Many shiny blades chopped the stalks into inch-long pieces. These pieces of corn shot up a pipe that extended to the top of the silo.

Louie ran inside the barn with Les at his heels. They climbed up a couple of steps of the silo and watched the corn pieces dropping from the pipe that Uncle Garrit was guiding at the bottom of the silo.

The boys quickly jumped down, and Louie headed for the cornfield. He wanted to be next to drive Harry Tanises' Doodlebug. He didn't have to wait long; soon Harry crossed the road toward the field. Louie jumped on the tongue of the wagon and rode behind Harry until they got to where the corn lay on the ground.

Harry jumped off, and Louie jumped on.

He put his foot on the clutch and put it in gear. Then he lifted his foot ever so carefully.

Oops! The Doodlebug lurched forward with a jerk. His head jerked back.

Harry laughed and said, "You'll get used to it."

Louie drove the Doodlebug from bundle to bundle of corn. Soon they had a load, and Louie gave up his seat to Harry, who drove the wagon of corn to the silo.

Harley and Louie each drove many makes of tractors throughout the day. They had a lot of fun, and the men were glad for the help.

The next week, the farmers went to another farm to fill another silo. The farmers depended on each other for help. They also enjoyed working together.

The Heifer

Louie didn't sleep very well one night that fall in 1948. He thought about the heifer, and he was filled with anticipation.

Harley and Cousin Hank came upon a dead Holstein heifer in the gully that afternoon. They had taken a shortcut through the gully on the way home from school.

A heifer is a young female cow. A Holstein is a black and white spotted breed.

Harley told Louie how it happened:

As we were walking home from school, we took a shortcut

through the gully. I was walking ahead of Hank down a cow path. I looked down the side of a hill and saw what looked like a Holstein cow lying on the hillside. Then I noticed it wasn't lying—it was hanging!

"Look!" I shouted. "A heifer got caught in the branches of that fallen down tree! She must have gotten stuck when she went down the hill."

Then I yelled, "That could be Dad's heifer! I better hurry home and tell him!"

Louie wondered, *How long has it been hanging in the tree? Was it Dad's heifer or Arnold Mater's? Both Dad and Arnold had Holstein heifers in that pasture.*

Arnold Mater lived across the field to the east of the Hooker farm on Comstock Avenue. His young cattle grazed on the grass in Uncle Garrit's gully, along with Dad's young cattle.

The next morning, before they could check out the heifer, the boys helped with the barn chores and cleaned under the chicken roosts.

When they finished, Dad fetched shovels and placed them in the trunk of the car.

Arnold and his son, Delty, met them at Uncle Garrit's house. They drove their cars across the old, rickety bridge behind the barn. The dead heifer hung in a tree behind the cornfield east of the bridge.

Arnold and Dad drove their cars down the lane right to the edge of the gully that stretched from Garret Sneller's farm.

Louie jumped out of the car, along with Harley and Les.

Louie ran ahead down the western slope of the gully. He peered across the gully. His eyes became fixed on a black-and-white carcass on the opposite side. Goose bumps rose on his neck as he looked through the trees.

"I see it right between those two trees. It's right over there!" shouted Louie as he pointed to the spot.

All the boys ran ahead toward the dead animal. They leaped across the creek at a narrow place and scampered up the slope to where it hung.

"Look at how it's wedged between those two limbs!" Delty yelled.

As Dad and Arnold walked up, Dad explained how the accident must have happened.

> The heifer must have thought the little opening between those two branches was a good place to get down the slope. She probably slipped and didn't realize the gap was too tight. She then began struggling, which wedged her tighter and tighter between the limbs. She couldn't get free and, in time, starved to death.

"Why don't we look at the tag on the heifer's ear?" Arnold suggested.

Farmers place a numbered tag on an ear of each calf. This is done to identify them. The tag number is written in the farmer's record book. The date of birth and the mother of the calf are also written in the book.

Arnold knelt on the ground, grabbed the tag, and read the number to Dad.

Dad wrote it on a sheet of paper.

Arnold pulled a little notebook from his pocket on which he had recorded his calves' numbers.

Dad grabbed a tablet from his pocket also.

Dad read the dead heifer's number out loud from the paper. "AC56932."

"That's my heifer!" Arnold shouted. "See the number here. It matches exactly to my Holstein calf that was born in the spring of 1947."

The dead heifer looked so much like Dad's. The only way to identify who it belonged to was by that number.

"I'm sorry, Arnold," Dad said. "It could have been mine."

"That's all right," he answered.

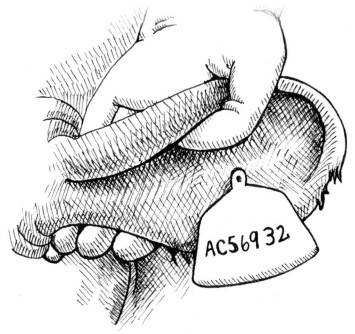

"Well, let's get to work and bury this carcass," Dad suggested.

Louie grabbed a shovel. Harley and Delty each grabbed one too.

"Where shall we make the hole?" Louie asked.

After looking carefully over the hillside, Dad and Arnold picked a site near the wedged carcass. First, Dad and Arnold each took an axe and chopped the limbs of the dead tree that held the heifer's body. It thudded to the ground near the place where Harley, Louie, and Delty were digging. The boys had to chop through tree roots and tough grass. At times, they removed large rocks from the hole.

After an hour, they had a hole about five feet deep and five feet wide. Louie's hands were sore, and he felt tired.

Louie rubbed the side of the heifer. Some hair stuck to his fingers. He shivered.

Everyone helped shove the dead animal in the hole, and all helped cover it with dirt.

As they traveled home, Dad said, "I'm happy my heifer is still alive, but I'm sad that Arnold's is dead. At least we worked together as friendly neighbors."

Geese Overhead

Later that fall, the north window in Harley and Louie's bedroom rattled. A strong north wind pelted little beads of ice against the window pane. It awakened Louie from a deep sleep. He lay still and tugged the quilt Mum had made from scraps of material tightly around his ears.

Honk! Honk! Honk! Those geese sounded like they were flying very low over the big white house.

Louie sat up and peered out the window. He couldn't see any ganders.

He wondered why they honked so loudly, even with the noisy wind.

Louie threw back the quilts and rushed down the stairway.

It was Saturday, so there was no hurry to get ready for school.

Dad stood by the dining room window, peering skyward. He heard the geese honking too.

"Wouldn't it be nice to have a fat goose for dinner tomorrow?" he said to Mum as she warmed herself by the dining room heat register.

"Yes, I could make a goose pie with a flaky crust," Mum answered.

"How are you going to shoot a goose?" Louie questioned as he stood at the bottom of the stairway.

"Oh, with buckshot and my twelve-gauge shotgun," Dad answered.

"Yeah, but they've already flown away!" Louie snapped.

Marve, Harley, and Les sat by the kitchen table, ready for breakfast. They were also all ears as Dad talked about shooting a goose. This was a rare event on the Hooker farm. Only on a windy day in November did this happen. The geese that migrated over the Hooker farm became confused when the wind blew strongly. This caused them to fly in a disorderly manner from farm to farm.

"Boys, eat some toast quickly while I get the gun ready. We have to hurry!" Dad shouted.

Louie grabbed two pieces of bread and stuck them in the toaster. He stood and waited for the bread so it wouldn't burn.

He quickly turned the toast around so the other side would brown also. The toaster had heat coils on only one side of the bread.

"Hurry, Louie," shouted Harley. "Or those geese will be gone!"

The boys bowed their heads for a quick prayer and gulped down their toast.

"I can't hear any honking. I wonder if they've flown too far away?" Louie said as he grabbed his coat and rushed out the door.

Dad stood just outside the door with his twelve-gauge shotgun in hand.

"Marve, you drive the car. Harley, Louie, and Les, get in the backseat. I'll sit beside Marve," Dad said.

As they headed down the driveway, Dad said, "Go toward the Hagens' and then east on Eightieth Street toward Uncle Garrit's place."

"Look!" Les shouted. "See that flock of geese way across the field toward the end of our property?"

Louie was looking out the window toward Uncle Garrit's and the gully.

"Yeah, that's them!" Marve hollered as he stepped harder on the gas pedal. Harley and Les leaned toward Louie's side of the car to get a glimpse of the confused flock of geese.

"Be careful, Marve," Dad warned as they rounded the corner onto Eightieth. "There might be some slippery spots of ice."

Marve peered intently out of the windshield. "There they go, straight toward Uncle Garrit's barn!" shouted Marve.

The car sped down the road toward Comstock Avenue.

"Oh, I think the birds are splitting up. Half of them are going back toward our place!" Les shouted.

"That's okay!" Dad yelled. "Keep going ahead and turn on Comstock, Marve!"

Marve drove the car right to where the gully crossed the road and pulled off to the side.

Dad and the boys jumped quickly from the car. Dad ran ahead toward the gully and said, "Boys, stay back. They're coming this way."

Dad popped a shell with buckshot into the gun.

The head goose let out a loud honk, and the others responded with their honks. They were flying right over Dad and quite high in the air.

Dad raised his gun and aimed toward the birds as they fluttered in confusion overhead.

Bang! Louie and Les were startled as they looked upward toward the flock.

A big gander, two back from the leader, stopped in midair and then fell, swirling toward the ground.

One or two of the BBs in the buckshot had hit the mark. The bird came tumbling down and hit the ground about fifty feet from Louie and Les. It never moved once it hit the ground. The boys hustled toward the dead bird.

It looked bigger when it was up in the sky. With both wings stretched out, the goose was wider than Les was tall.

Louie grabbed one of its wings and stretched it out.

"Boy! This goose sure has wide wings!" Louie said as he stretched it even farther. The goose was mostly gray and brown in color, with a black neck and a white spot under its chin. It was a Canada goose.

They all gathered around and examined the fallen bird. The boys were proud of their dad, who was such a sure shot.

"Harley, get the bag from the trunk of the car. We'll put the goose in the bag so it doesn't make the trunk dirty," Dad commanded.

Harley rushed away as Marve picked up the heavy goose. "I think it weighs at least twenty pounds," he remarked as he carried it toward the car. "This sure ought to make some good goose pie."

That night, Dad skinned the goose. He used a sharp knife that Mum used when peeling potatoes. It was too hard to pluck the feathers because the down was too thick for hot, scalding water to penetrate. The goose meat was a dark red color, and Dad cut it into small pieces.

Louie's mouth watered as he imagined the smell of the delicious goose pie that Mum would make the next day. She always made the crust so flaky and delicious.

Dad's Smelly Story

December 1948 arrived. The cold north winds brought snow. Louie and his brothers and sisters spent more time inside the big white house.

Louie looked forward to Sunday afternoon after church. Dad often sat at the dining room table and told or read stories.

On this Sunday, Les, Harley, and Louie sat on the floor near Dad's chair. Corrine, Dale, and Barbie sat nearby on chairs.

Dad began telling his story:

When I was a teenager, I would trap muskrats and mink. I would sell their furs to make money. I went down to the creek behind our barn, where many muskrats lived.

"How would you know where to put the traps?" Louie interrupted.

"Oh, we looked for tracks and signs where muskrats had walked," Dad answered.

Dad continued his story.

Well, anyway, we found many places where we knew muskrats lived. We had to remember where we placed the traps so we could find them the next day.

Early the next morning before school, while it was still dark, Uncle Joe and I set out to check the trap line. The first two traps had muskrats caught by their feet. We thought we were going to have a successful morning.

The next five or six traps had nothing.

When we approached the final trap, we heard a rustling of the leaves where the trap was located near the creek bank.

The first rays of sunlight were just beginning to appear in the eastern sky.

Uncle Joe and I slowly approached the trap and the animal trying to free itself from the jaws of the trap.

"I see something white!" Joe shouted.

Then we heard a soft snorting sound.

"Oh, I think it's a skunk!" I hollered.

I remembered a friend at school told me how to treat a skunk so you wouldn't get sprayed.

My friend told me if you hit the skunk on his back with a big stick, he couldn't spray. So I hunted for and found a strong stick nearby. I crept cautiously toward the entrapped skunk while Joe stood nearby and watched. The skunk tried desperately to escape. Just as he looked away from me, I swung my stick with all my might. I hit him right in the middle of the back.

Just as I hit him, a yellow spray flew at me from the skunk.

"Oh, he got me right in my face!" I shouted. "Ouch! My eyes!"

I quickly grabbed some snow and rubbed my stinging eyes. The snow in my hand turned yellow when I rubbed my face. The smell was horrible.

"Let's go home! I've got to clean my face and get rid of the stink!" I shouted.

We hustled home and put the three muskrats in a pail in the milk house. We had to hurry to clean up and go to school. I took a bath and washed my face the best I could.

After a quick breakfast, we hurried out the door. We had to walk a mile and a half to Brookside School. When we got there, I told my friends the thrilling story of the skunk.

The bell rang. We went inside and took our seats.

When the teacher checked to see who was present, he stopped suddenly and said, "Who smells like a skunk?"

Everyone looked at me. I was so embarrassed.

He told me I would have to go home and get rid of the smell.

So I walked home, took another bath, and scrubbed my face very carefully.

I went back to school at noon. The teacher and class said I smelled a lot better.

"Tell us another story!" Corrine cried.

"No," Dad said. "We'll have to wait until next week. It's time for chores."

America, the Land of the Free

The next Sunday in the late afternoon, Louie and the rest of the kids gathered around Dad for another story. Louie's brother, Marve, was also there. Virginia was off to college in Grand Rapids.

Dad began reading a book he had gotten from the church library. The book was about a pioneer family that emigrated from the Netherlands to Holland, Michigan, during the 1840s.

The first winter after they arrived was very cold and snowy. The family, being very poor, often went hungry.

Dad read from the book:

Father wondered if there was enough food to get them through the next week.

When Mother tucked little Johnnie into bed that night, she noticed his frail arms.

Greta whimpered, "I'm hungry," as she lay her tiny head on the pillow.

Dad paused briefly from his reading. He asked the kids, "How would you like to live at the time of Johnnie and Greta?"

Corrine piped up, "I'm glad we have lots of jars of food in the basement."

Barbie chimed in, "I like Mum's peaches and apple sauce."

At that moment Brownie barked from the little kitchen as he heard a passing car on the road.

Louie added, "I like metwurst and Mum's goose pie."

Les sat quietly thinking about Dad's question and said, "I'm glad that Dad has a tractor to do the farm work and not just horses."

The furnace in the basement made a pinging noise as the pipes warmed up.

"How about you, Harley?" asked Dad.

Harley scratched his head as he thought for a moment. "We have a furnace and lots of wood piled by the barnyard fence to keep us warm through the winter."

Then Dale burst out, "I'm glad Dad grows lots of potatoes so Mum can make yummy scalloped potatoes."

Marve said, "I'm sure happy we have cars so we don't have to ride horses or walk everywhere we go."

Mum sat crocheting in her rocking chair, smiling as she listened to her children's answers to Dad's question.

"Yes, God has been good to us," said Dad. "We can be thankful that we live during the 1940s in America, the land of the free."

The winter sun was setting in the west, and the animals were snug in their barn and coops.

Louie felt contented as comforting, warm air flowed from the furnace below. The Hooker family continued to listen as Dad read the story about Johnnie and Greta.

Contact Information

Louis Hooker
6900 Chamberlain
Fremont, MI 49412
lvhook@ncats.net